PADDINGTON BEAR

Acknowledgment is made to Peggy Fortnum,
who first illustrated Paddington Bear.

CIP data may be found at the end of the book.

Paddington Bear

by

MICHAEL BOND

illustrated by

FRED BANBERY

RANDOM HOUSE
NEW YORK

First American Edition 1973. Text Copyright © 1972 by Michael Bond.
Illustrations Copyright © 1972 by Fred Banbery.
All rights reserved under International and Pan-American Copyright
Conventions. Published in the United States by Random House, Inc.,
New York. Originally published in Great Britain by William Collins
Sons & Co., Ltd., London.
Manufactured in the United States of America.

One day Mr. and Mrs. Brown were standing in Paddington station. They were waiting for their daughter Judy who was coming home from school. Suddenly Mr. Brown noticed something small and furry behind a pile of mailbags.

"Look over there," he said to Mrs. Brown.
"I'm sure I saw a bear."

"*A bear?*" said Mrs. Brown. "In Paddington station? Don't be silly, Henry. There can't be."

But there was. It had a funny kind of hat and it was sitting all by itself on an old suitcase near the Lost Property Office.

7

As they drew near, the bear stood up and politely raised its hat. "Good afternoon," it said, in a small clear voice. "Can I help you?"

"We were wondering if *we* could help *you*,"
said Mrs. Brown. "Wherever have you
come from?"

The bear looked round carefully before replying. "*Darkest* Peru. I stowed away and I lived on marmalade!"

Mrs. Brown spied a label round the bear's neck. It said simply: PLEASE LOOK AFTER THIS BEAR. THANK YOU. AUNT LUCY.

"Henry," she exclaimed, "we shall have to take him home with us."

"But we don't even know his name," began Mr. Brown.

"We'll call him Paddington," said Mrs. Brown.
"Because that's where we found him."

Mrs. Brown went off to look for Judy and
Mr. Brown took Paddington into the
cafeteria for something to eat.

He left Paddington sitting at a corner table
near the window. He soon returned carrying
two steaming cups of tea and a large plate piled
high with sticky cakes.

After his long journey Paddington felt so
hungry and thirsty he didn't know which to
do first—eat or drink.

"I think I'll try both at the same time if you
don't mind, Mr. Brown," he announced.

And without waiting for a reply he climbed
up onto the table. Mr. Brown stared out of the
window, pretending he had tea with a bear at
Paddington station every day of his life.

When Mrs. Brown came into the cafeteria
with Judy she threw up her hands in horror.

"Henry," she said. "What *are* you doing to
that poor bear? He's covered all over with
cream and jam."

At the sound of Mrs. Brown's voice Paddington
jumped so much he stepped on a patch of
strawberry jam and fell over backwards into
his saucer of tea.

"I think we'd better go before anything else happens," said Mr. Brown. And he quickly led the way out of the cafeteria.

Judy took Paddington's paw and squeezed it.

"Come along," she said.
"We'll take you home in
a taxi. Then you can
have a nice hot bath
and meet my brother
Jonathan."

Paddington had never been in a taxi before.
He found it very exciting and he stood on a

little tip-up seat behind the driver so that he could wave to the people in the street.

Soon they pulled up outside a large house with a green front door.

When they were indoors Judy took Paddington
up to his room to unpack.

"I haven't got very much," said Paddington.
"Only some marmalade. . .

. . . and my scrapbook . . .

. . . and a sort of South American penny."

He held up
a photograph.
"And that's my
Aunt Lucy.
She had it taken
just before she went
into the Home for
Retired Bears."

Next Judy showed Paddington to the bathroom.

As soon as he was on his own he turned on the taps and then climbed onto a stool in order to look out of the window.

Then he tried writing his name on the steamy glass with his paw. It took him rather a long time and when he looked round he found to his surprise that the bath was so full of water it was starting to run over the side.

He closed his eyes, and, holding his nose with
one paw, he jumped in.

The water was hot, soapy, and very deep,
and to his horror he found he couldn't get out.
He couldn't even see to turn the taps off.

Paddington tried calling out "Help"—at first
in a quiet voice, so as not to disturb anyone
and then much louder, "HELP! HELP!"

But still nobody came.

Then he had an idea.

He took off his hat and began using it to
bail out the water.

Downstairs, Judy was telling her brother all about Paddington.

Suddenly, she felt a PLOP.

Looking up she saw a dark, wet patch on the ceiling.

"Paddington!" she cried. "He must be in trouble. Quick!"

And together they raced out of the room.

Jonathan and Judy leaned over the side of the
bath and lifted a dripping and very frightened
Paddington on to the floor.

"What a mess!" said Jonathan. "We'd better
wipe it up pretty quickly."

"Oh, Paddington," said Judy. "What good
luck we found you in time. You might have
drowned."

Paddington sat up. "What good luck I had
my hat," he said.

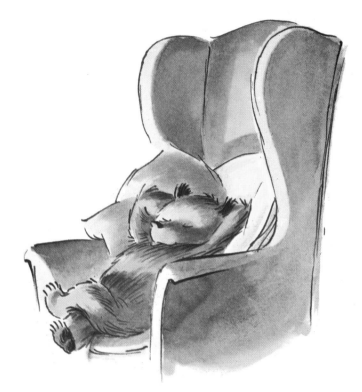

Some time later a beautifully clean Paddington
came downstairs. Settling himself down in a
small armchair by the fire, he put his paws
behind his head and stretched out his toes.

It was nice being a bear – especially a bear
called Paddington. He had a feeling that life
with the Browns was going to be fun.